The Goblin Princess

The
Grand
Goblin
Ball

The Goblin Princess

The Grand Goblin Ball

Jenny O'Connor

illustrated by
Kate Willis-Crowley

FABER & FABER

First published in 2017
by Faber & Faber Limited
Bloomsbury House,
74–77 Great Russell Street,
London WC1B 3DA

A CIP record for this book is available from the British Library

Printed in China

978–0571–31660–1

2 4 6 8 10 9 7 5 3 1

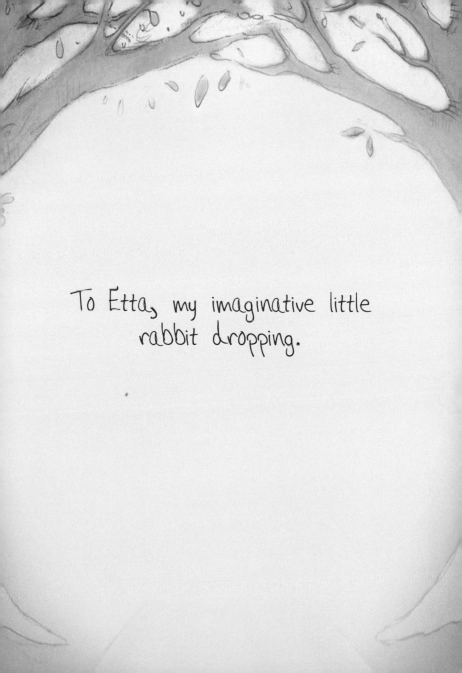

To Etta, my imaginative little
rabbit dropping.

Crystal
Isles

Port
Barnacle

Bagstock
Village

Goblin
Castle

Ogre
Mountains

Chapter 1

Party Invitations

SPLAT! Mrs Dollop was giving the Goblin Castle its annual spring dirtying. Matty, the Goblin Princess, was running down the stone stairs with Smoky, her pet dragon, when they were suddenly enveloped in a huge cloud of dust.

'Hello, my little rabbit dropping,'

 1

said Mrs Dollop. 'I'm just getting the place ready for tonight's party.'

The Goblin Queen frowned. 'Mrs Dollop! Stop gossiping. There's still so much work to be done. Now, Matty, you'll have to entertain yourself today. Your father's just gone off to post all the invitations for the Grand Goblin Ball, and I have to help Mrs Dollop dress up the cake.'

'Can I invite my friends?' asked Prince Stinkwort, Matty's brother. He was managing to slide down the stair bannister, chew on a particularly slimy

slug, and talk all at the same time!

'Of course you can, Stinkwort. Everyone in the Goblin Kingdom will get an invitation. Except, of course, the horrible hobgoblins. They certainly aren't invited. Now, who will you invite, Matty?' asked the Goblin Queen.

'Matty hasn't got any friends. **BURP!**' Stinkwort belched loudly.

Matty stared at her feet miserably.

'**Burp! Plop!**' Princess Plop copied her brother.

The Queen looked down fondly at her baby daughter and wiped a bit more

dirt on to her face. 'Well done, Plop.
Matty, my little horribleness, why can't
you burp like your brother and sister? I
know you're not like most goblins, but
if only you behaved a bit more like a
goblin should, you'd have lots of friends.
Could you try at least to *like* eating
slugs?'

'I fwiend,' said
Smoky softly.

'I know,
Smoky.' Matty
stroked her pet
dragon.

Smoky suddenly ran to
the window, his little blue tail
wagging wildly. 'Look, Smatty!'

'Your dragon looks like he wants
to go out for a walk, my little puppy
doo-doo,' said Mrs Dollop kindly.

But looking up, Matty could see
what she knew no other goblin in the
kingdom could. There was a fairy at
the window! Fern, her very own fairy
friend from Raven Wood, had come to
see her!

Matty whispered a warning to her
pet dragon. 'Shh, Smoky. Nobody

would believe that we
can see fairies!'

Fern looked like a
tiny ball of sparkling
light as she flew through

the open window. Matty could just
make out her pretty face and delicate
clothes. The fairy flew straight up to
Smoky and gave him a kiss, her long
hair and swirling skirt of miniature
fern leaves flying out behind her.

'Matty, close that window! You're
letting all the dust out,' said the Goblin
Queen, blissfully unaware that a little

fairy was now sitting
on her crown looking
curiously down at her.
'Well, Mrs Dollop,
we must get on. The
castle has to look its
very worst. We need
to untidy every room
and bring in some more
dust. And where are the
cobwebs? What useless
spiders we seem to have! Go out into
the garden and catch some more, could
you, Stinkwort?'

'Oooh, I'll get out the dustblower, Your Gobness. Nothing spreads the dirt as fast,' said Mrs Dollop, fetching her favourite machine from the depths of a messy cupboard.

When the goblins had left, Matty opened the palm of her hand to let Fern rest on it. 'It's so good to see you. Where are Teasel and Tansy?'

'That's why I've come,' Fern replied. 'They're missing, Matty. Have you seen them?'

Matty shook her head. 'I haven't. Have you, Smoky?'

'Cwumbs, no!'

Fern was fretful. 'They went out this morning very early after breakfast and didn't come back for lunch. I'm really worried – they've never missed a meal before. I wondered if they had come to visit you at the Goblin Castle.'

Matty was dismayed. 'No, they haven't, Fern. How can I help?'

Fern sighed. 'If the twins arrive at the castle, tell them to come home straightaway. I can't stay, Matty. I'm sorry. I'll have to carry on looking.'

So Matty waved goodbye to Fern,

watched her fly away across the messy castle grounds, then slowly closed the window. 'Oh, Smoky. This is dreadful!'

'Dweadful!' agreed the dragon, his tail drooping sorrowfully.

Chapter 2

Plans Afoot

Teasel and Tansy's adventure had started harmlessly enough. The two fairies were playing chase, following a flight of pretty pink butterflies through Raven Wood. It was so much fun dashing through the leaves that neither noticed when they reached the

end of the wood and came to the lower
reaches of Hob Mountain.

'They went this way,' laughed Teasel,
following a crimson butterfly through
a dark tangle of trees. The two fairies
swooped down through the branches
but found, to their surprise, that the

butterflies had disappeared. The fairies
seemed to be in a strange rocky shaft.
Intrigued, they inched forward.

'What's this?' said Teasel.

'We're in a cave!' Tansy replied.

'Let's explore!' they said together.

It was fun exploring the maze of
underground tunnels that led away
from the cave. But the tunnels soon
became damp and dark. After a while,

the two fairies longed to be outside
in the fresh air. Turning around, they
started to make their way back.

'Was it this way?' asked Teasel,
pointing to a curved tunnel on the right.

'No, I think it was over to the left,'
suggested Tansy. They flew through
tunnel after tunnel but eventually the
twins had to admit that they were lost.

'What's that strange smell?' asked
Tansy.

The two fairies sniffed the air. There
was a strange smoky smell.

'Let's follow the scent. It might lead us to the outside.' The twins flew along the dark tunnels towards the smell of cooking, but it didn't lead them outside. It led them to a gloomy cavern at the heart of Hob Mountain –

straight to where the hobgoblins lived!
The hobgoblins were gathered around
a smoky fire, munching on nettle
and bacon sandwiches and making
troublesome plans.

Commander Spike was talking,

spitting out pieces of bacon with every word. 'Tonight is the night of the Grand Ball at the Goblin Castle. There'll be music, dancing, feasting and food fights. And where will we be? I'll tell you. We'll be staying right here, boys, because we're not invited.'

'**Booo!**' cried the other hobgoblins, shaking their grey fists at the unfairness of it all.

'Fear not, fellow hobgoblins. I have a plan that will wipe the smug smiles right off the faces of the goblin royal family.' Triumphantly, Spike produced a

yellowing map from the pocket of his dirty trousers.

The other hobgoblins cackled wildly and stamped their hobnailed boots. 'Tell us, Spike! Don't keep us in suspense.'

Spike lowered his voice to a near-whisper, and leant in towards the listening horde. 'Very few know this, but there are secret tunnels beneath the castle. Tunnels that lead from the deepest caves in Hob Mountain to the very heart of the Goblin Castle.'

There were gasps
of amazement from Spike's
audience, but he raised his hand for
silence. Pointing to the map, he went
on. 'This evening, we'll make our way
along these tunnels. Then, at the stroke
of midnight, we'll storm the party.'

'What will we do when we get
inside?' asked One-Eyed Spud.

'I'll tell you what we're going to do,'
chuckled Spike, rubbing his hands
together gleefully. 'As soon as we get in,
the big'uns will hold the party guests
back while the rest of us will . . . *clean*

the castle! Sweep the floors. Dust the walls! Blow away the cobwebs! Give it a thorough **SPRING CLEAN!**'

The group gasped at the outrageous idea. A little hobgoblin at the back of the group nearly fainted in shock.

'We might even . . .' Spike paused dramatically, '. . . give it a . . . *lick of paint!*'

Old Spud, his one eye glinting mischievously, roared with laughter. 'Brilliant notion, Spike. Paint it! I've never heard anything so dastardly!'

A small nervous hobgoblin shuffled

forward. 'S-s-steady on, S-S-Spike!
Cleaning the place up will be bad
enough. The royal family will never get
over it. They'll be the laughing stock
of the goblin world. But . . . a lick of
paint? That's going too f-f-far!'

'Well, perhaps you're right, Trotter.
We're rotten rascals but we're not that
cruel. There *is* one more thing I want to
do though.'

'What's that, Spike?'

'Capture that piddling little dragon
that belongs to the Goblin Princess. The
one that got away from me in Raven

Wood. I want to put him to work heating these draughty tunnels with his fire-breathing. It's too cold in here!'

Excited chatter broke out amongst the hobgoblins at the news of Spike's daring plan. 'We'll show 'em. Not invite us, will they? We'll give them a party they'll never forget.'

As the hobgoblins' cackles rang out around the cave, the two little fairies looked at one another, appalled.

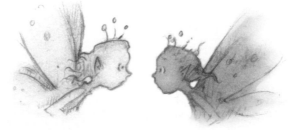

'We have to warn Matty. There's no time to lose,' whispered Tansy to her twin sister.

Teasel spoke softly. Although she was certain that fairies were invisible to the hobgoblins, she had no idea if they could be heard. 'Yes, but first we have to go home to Raven Wood. Fern will be worrying about where we've got to. Though before we can do anything at all, we have to find a way to escape!'

Chapter 3

The Grand Goblin Ball

That evening the castle was looking its filthy worst. Everything was ready for the Grand Goblin Ball. Mrs Dollop had made sure that every surface was thick with dust and grime. The new spiders that Prince Stinkwort had found in the garden had done their

best work and cobwebs were
hanging from every corner.

'Oooh, everything looks so
grubby,' cried Mrs Dollop with relish.

The King, though,
looked worried.
'I think we need
security tonight.
The hobgoblins
won't be
happy that
we haven't
sent them an
invitation.

What if they try to join us?'

'I'll get Mr Dollop on to it, Your Gobness,' said the ever-helpful castle cook. 'He can patrol the castle grounds tonight. No one will get past Mr Dollop.'

'Really?' asked the King doubtfully.

Matty was watching the Goblin Queen put the finishing touches to her startling party outfit.

'I've just been to the hair-messers. How do I look?' asked the Queen.

'Er, you look, well . . . revolting,'

said Matty, looking uncertainly at her mother's fungus-encrusted gown.

The Queen beamed. 'Flatterer! Thank you, Matty. Now for the finishing touches.' She sprayed herself with her favourite perfume, Eau de Slime Pond, and added a few fake warts to her face. 'I want to look my very worst tonight,' the Queen told her daughter. Seeing Matty's face, she added, 'Don't look so worried, Matty. One day you'll

have warts of your own.
You'll grow out of those
good looks, I'm sure.
You might even get to
look as ugly as me!'

But Matty wasn't
worried about warts. She
was worried about Teasel
and Tansy. Wherever
could they be?

Outside in the hall, the
old grandgoblin clock
struck eight.

'Eight o'clock already! The guests will be arriving soon,' cried the Queen. She surveyed her dirty, dishevelled family. 'You all look disgusting. I'm so proud of you!'

CLANG!
CLANG!
CLANG!

Mr Dollop, dressed in an ancient suit of rusty armour, clanked slowly towards the front door. 'I will start my patrol of the castle grounds,' he said solemnly. The old castle door creaked open and Mr Dollop rattled outside.

'EIGHT O'CLOCK AND ALL'S SMELL!' came his watchman's cry.

In the caves of Hob Mountain, the Hobgoblin Army was gathering.

'Mops at the ready, men,' said Commander Spike.

31

'Yes, Spike!' chorused the hobgoblins.

Dozens of hobgoblins armed with brooms, mops, buckets and dusters gathered around their leader.

'They won't know what hit 'em. Have you got the dragon cage ready, Trotter?'

'Yes, Spike.'

'Good. I'm going to enjoy watching that mingy squirt of a dragon learn his lesson. No one escapes from Spike twice!'

Teasel, watching from the shadows, had a plan. 'We'll have to follow the hobgoblins to the castle, Tansy.'

'NINE O'CLOCK AND ALL'S SMELL!'

At the castle, guests were starting to arrive. They came from all over the Goblin Kingdom. There were business goblins in their tatty suits, hair-messers, window-dirtiers with their buckets full of eggs, the workgoblins who kept the roads full of potholes, grubby teachers with rows of grubby schoolgoblins, bedraggled families with gloopy babies. They poured in through the gates and through the huge castle door, each one proudly holding their sticky green invitation.

'Look, Smoky! There's Miss Grimwig the dragon untrainer, with her naughty dragon, Slobber,' said Matty.

'Cwipes, Smatty!' Smoky hid behind the Goblin Princess.

The Goblin Princess giggled. 'Don't worry, Smoky. Miss Grimwig won't be testing you again for naughty dragon potential. She gave you up as a hopeless case. I just hope Slobber doesn't burn the party decorations!'

In the great green ballroom of the Goblin Castle, a magnificent spread of goblin food had been laid out on the ancient banqueting tables. There were worm pasties, spider-leg sandwiches, slime stew, maggot pies and wobbling frogspawn jellies.

'Grub's up!' called Mrs Dollop,
pushing an escaping maggot back on
to one of the serving plates. The royal
family and hordes of party guests
sat down to eat the feast. Matty was
relieved to find that Mrs Dollop had
made her some insect-free rice and
vegetable pasties. The old cook didn't
approve of Matty's strange tastes
but she wasn't going to let the young

princess go hungry at the Goblin Ball.

The feast began and the goblins found Mrs Dollop's cooking so delicious that for a while the only sounds that could be heard were the slurps and satisfied belches of the party-goers.

Then the King stood up and banged his spoon. 'Before the food fights begin, we have some thrilling entertainment for you all!'

Smoky, who had been getting scraps of food from Matty under the table, heard the goblins' excited whispers. 'Gerrump!' he said, peeking from underneath the tablecloth.

An excited murmur went around the room as the huge double doors flew open. A tall thin goblin, carrying a whip and wearing a top hat, walked smartly into the ballroom and bowed

to his audience. Four assistant
goblins followed him,
carrying a miniature
green circus tent.
Every goblin in
the room stopped
eating and leant
forward.

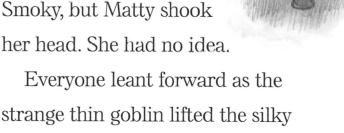

'Whatssat?' asked
Smoky, but Matty shook
her head. She had no idea.

Everyone leant forward as the
strange thin goblin lifted the silky
curtain of the circus tent. A gold tooth

glinted when he spoke. 'Good evening. My name is Mr Froggit. Please allow me to introduce, for your slimy delight and entertainment, the croaky, green and slippery . . . *Amazing Frog Circus*!'

And out they hopped! Hundreds of little squelchy frogs, marching to the croaky sound of a frog orchestra.

The goblins went wild!

They cheered, clapped
and stamped their
feet. There were frog clowns, little
green trapeze artists, acrobats and
ballerinas. There was even a large fat
strong toad lifting heavy weights and
croaking with pride. The goblins were
entranced.

Matty lifted Smoky on to her lap so he could get a better view of the circus show.

'Fwogs!' he cried happily.

'TEN O'CLOCK AND ALL'S SMELL!'

Far below them, the Hobgoblin Army marched towards the party, the sound of their hobnailed boots ringing out in the gloomy tunnel.

44

'Quickly,' whispered Teasel to her twin sister. 'We know their awful plan. We have to keep up so we can warn Matty in time.'

Chapter 4

Dave, Frog of Mystery and Magic

'And now for our grand finale,' said Mr Froggit to his goblin audience. 'I am proud to introduce the incredible, the sensational, the *fantastical* . . . Dave, Frog of Mystery and Magic!'

A spotlight shone down on to the

stage as a small frog
hopped forward, dressed
in a purple magician's
hat and holding a
magic wand.

Dave blinked
nervously and cleared
his throat. 'F-f-for
m-my first trick I will
fill the bowl you see before you with
sprouts.' He paused, waited for silence,
and then waved his magic wand.

'*Fartberries of the straw*, Sproutus
Explodus!'

The goblins all licked their lips. Sprouts! What a treat! The crowd gasped as the bowl lit up with sparks and stars.

KAPOW!

Then turned into . . . a bowl of juicy strawberries!

'**BOOO!**' cried the horrified audience. 'Strawberries! Disgusting! I think I'm going to be sick! Where are our sprouts? Off, off, **OFF!**'

Dave looked around nervously at Mr Froggit, who glared thunderously back at him.

SQUELCH! Somebody  threw a frogspawn jelly at the poor frog magician. Dave wiped the quivering gloop from his eyes and saw Mr Froggit advancing, brandishing a sharp pointy stick. With a giant leap, Dave jumped off the stage and landed right by the Goblin Princess.

'WHERE IS THAT DRATTED FROG?' raged Mr Froggit, peering into the dark audience.

Without thinking, Matty threw her handkerchief over Dave. 'Shh! Keep quiet.'

The goblins searched the hall but couldn't find the frog anywhere.

'He's done a disappearing trick!' suggested someone in the audience.

'It would be the first time any of

his tricks actually worked!' laughed
another.

Underneath Matty's handkerchief,
Dave quaked in fear. 'RRRR-BITT!' he
cried, in panic.

The noise was loud, and everyone
in the hall turned to face
Matty. There was a
terrible silence. The
Goblin Princess
put her hand to her
mouth in horror.

The Goblin King
saved the little frog without realising it.

'Well done, Matty. That was a burp any goblin would be proud of!'

'Thanks, Dad,' said Matty gratefully. She picked up her handkerchief, folding it around the frog, and put both in her pocket. Dave, snuggled in the safety of Matty's skirt, gave a quiet croak of relief.

'Smatty, look!'

'What is it, Smoky?'

Matty looked to where the dragon pup was pointing. Two little twinkling lights were flying over the heads of the party guests, towards her table.

Fairies? At the Grand Goblin Ball?

As they came closer, Matty could see that it was Teasel and Tansy. They were safe! Smoky yipped with delight but Matty put a steadying hand on his head. 'Shh,' she whispered. 'No one can know they're here.'

But the moment she saw their faces, Matty knew that the twins hadn't come to enjoy the party. The fairies flew down to whisper in her ear. 'Come quickly, Matty. The castle is about to be attacked – you're all in terrible danger!'

Chapter 5

The Castle Vaults

'Come on, Smoky.' Matty, her heart pounding, quietly got up and followed the fairies to the hall outside. The food fights had started, and pasties, pies and jellies were flying everywhere! In all the

confusion, nobody noticed
Matty and Smoky slip away.

The old grandgoblin
clock struck eleven.

Teasel, her face serious for once,
explained. 'The hobgoblins are hiding
in tunnels below the castle. They were
angry that they weren't invited to
the ball. At midnight they're going
to invade the castle and . . . and . . .'
Teasel hesitated, afraid to go on.
'Clean it!' she whispered, fearfully.

'Clean it!' gasped Matty.

'Yes,' said the two fairies grimly. 'Clean it.'

'And there's worse. They also want to kidnap Smoky.'

'Yelp!' said Smoky.

Matty gasped in horror but she knew she had to be brave. She squeezed her pet dragon tightly. 'Thank you for coming to warn me, but now you two should go straight back home. Fern's out looking for you. She's very worried. I'm so relieved that you're safe.'

'But Smoky's not safe, Matty. The

hobgoblins want to kidnap him to heat their caves! We have to stop them,' said Teasel.

'**RIBBITT!**' The noise came from Matty's pocket.

'What's that?' asked Tansy.

The little frog peeked out from the folds of Matty's skirt, looked round cautiously to check that his cruel master was

nowhere to be seen, and then hopped out on to Matty's lap. Lifting his little magician's hat, he bowed solemnly. 'I am Dave, Frog of Mystery and Magic,' he told the astonished fairies.

'Dave was part of Mr Froggit's Frog Circus, but his magic trick went wrong,' Matty explained.

Dave indignantly puffed out his chest. 'I perform wonderful tricks. They just don't always turn out as I plan.'

'Nice to meet you, Dave,' said Tansy.

Teasel flew round their heads impatiently. 'Come on. We have to stop the hobgoblins!'

'Where are they now?' asked Matty.

 58

'We'll show you!'

Matty followed the fairies down the long winding staircase that led to the dark vaults of the Goblin Castle. Dave hopped on to Smoky's back and held on tightly as the little dragon rushed down the stone stairs after his mistress.

'It's so dark down here. I can hardly see,' said Matty.

'Allow me,' croaked Dave, pointing to an old unlit lantern sitting in a nook in the wall. Waving his wand, the little frog chanted his spell.

'*Bang on the light,* Desausagio*!*'

Matty held her breath. There was an explosion of twinkling stars and a heap of sausages tumbled on to the stairs.

'Oh no, now we have bangers!' groaned Dave. 'Scwummy!'

Smoky wagged his little tail and gobbled up a sausage.

Seeing the frog's disappointed face, Matty tried to reassure him. 'Never mind, Dave. Smoky can make fire, can't you, Smoky?

The little dragon, his mouth full of sausage, didn't look too sure. He hadn't been named Smoky for nothing.

Most of his efforts produced tiny puffs
of white smoke, not fire.

'Go on, Smoky. You can do it if you
really try. Maybe eating that tasty
sausage will help.'

'Smoky help Smatty.' Smoky drew
in a deep breath. His little face grew
pink with concentration. Suddenly a
lick of flame shot towards the candle

in the lantern and lit it.

'Hurrah!' they all cheered. 'Well done, Smoky! We have light!'

Now, armed with the flickering lantern, the friends dashed down the remaining stairs towards a large ancient wooden door.

'This is it! We're at the bottom. This is the door that leads into the secret passages,' explained Tansy.

Matty tried the rusty handle. 'The door's locked. How did you get through it?'

'We flew in through the keyhole,'

explained Teasel. 'I know that the hobgoblins are planning on battering the door down.'

'Well, it's hopeless then. How on earth will *we* be able get through?' cried Matty desperately.

'Erm, perhaps I could magic us smaller?' suggested Dave hopefully.

'Really?' said Matty, but seeing Dave's crestfallen face, she added encouragingly, 'Give it a try, Dave. You're our only chance.'

The little frog had never felt so needed in his life. Dave jumped on to

Smoky's head and took a deep breath.

Once again he waved his tiny wand.

'*Mini us,* Explodium*!*'

There was a blast of twinkling stars.

'Eeek!' peeped Smoky nervously.

BOOOOOOOM!

There was a huge flash of light
followed by strange purple smoke.
The explosion made them cough but
it didn't make them smaller.

'Sorry,' croaked Dave.

Matty looked around at everyone. 'It's hopeless. There's just no way we can get into that secret passage.'

'I think we can, Matty,' gasped Teasel. 'The explosion has blown out the lock in the door!'

Chapter 6

Into the Secret Tunnels

Matty carefully pushed open the door to the secret tunnel and put a finger to her lips. 'We'll have to be really quiet,' she whispered.

Silently, they all inched forward.

Teasel pointed further up the tunnel. 'Hold the lantern up high, Matty.

I think the hobgoblins are just
up ahead.'

Outside in the castle grounds, Mr
Dollop continued his watch.

'TWELVE O'CLOCK AND ALL'S SMELL!'

'How much longer do we have to
wait?' One-Eyed Spud was impatient
for the attack to start. Unknown to the
others, he'd put a pot of paint and a
paintbrush in his pocket, and he wasn't
afraid to use them.

'I've told you. Thirteen o'clock! By then the food fights will be in full swing. No one will be suspecting the Hobgoblin Clean-Up Force!'

'W-what's th-that, Spike?' Trotter had pointed a trembling finger further up the tunnel. Coming towards them was a flickering light. Matty's lantern was casting an enormous shadow of her and Smoky on to the tunnel wall. The rabble of hobgoblins turned wide-eyed with horror as the two huge shadows advanced towards them.

'It's a giant!'

It's a forest troll!

'It's a two-headed monster!'

'It's an *enormous* dragon!'

'**RUN!**' And the Hobgoblin Army,
their brooms and buckets clanging
in the darkness, fled back up
the passageway.

Matty saw the fleeing hobgoblins ahead of them. 'Look! The light of the lantern has made our shadows look like huge monsters! They're running away!'

'Yippee!' said Teasel. 'Let's follow them. We should make sure that they're really going home.'

'Good idea. Come on, Smoky!'

'Okey-smoky!' puffed the little dragon.

The tunnel ahead split into two directions. 'Which path did they take?' asked Matty.

'Ribbitt! This narrower one, I think,' croaked Dave.

One-Eyed Spud wasn't happy that the raid had been abandoned. 'Wait up, wait up! Stop, you lot! We're the heroic Hobgoblin Clean-Up Force! Why are we running away?'

'Because there w-was a giant and a g-giant d-dragon,' said the quaking Trotter, as they came to a halt.

'But there are dozens of us. A match for any monster!'

A murmur went round the hobgoblin horde. 'One-Eyed Spud is right. We're a force to be reckoned with. Giant or no giant! Let's get 'em!'

Once Commander Spike had got his breath back, he spoke up. 'A hobgoblin afraid of a giant and his dragon? Ridiculous! Soapsuds at the ready, hobgoblins! CHARGE!'

Holding their brooms and mops aloft, the hobgoblins tore back towards the Goblin Castle. They stopped when they reached the fork in the tunnel.

Commander Spud made a decision.

 75

'The castle is straight ahead but there's a light down there in the narrower tunnel. It's probably the lair of the monster and his dragon. Come on, lads. Let's go and finish them off before we storm the castle.'

'Yeah!' roared the naughty hobgoblins.

'The narrow tunnel was the wrong one. We seem to have come to a dead end,' said Matty as the friends looked at the stone wall in front of them.

'Never mind, we'll just go back,' said Teasel.

'Uh oh – no we won't!' gasped Tansy. Turning around, Matty and her friends saw to their horror that a troop of hobgoblins had appeared and were moving menacingly towards them.

'We're trapped!' she squeaked.

Spike smiled cruelly. 'Well, well. Look what we have here! A monster and his dragon, eh, Trotter? I don't think so. A Goblin Princess, a frog and her pathetic little pet. Fetch the dragon cage. I think it's time to take our first prisoner.'

'Cwumbs!' Smoky tried to hide behind his mistress's legs.

'Dave?' whispered Matty. 'Have you *ever* managed to get a magic trick right?'

'No,' admitted Dave, sadly.

'Perhaps it's time to really, *really* try.'

A grey hand had reached forward to grab the poor trembling Smoky, when a determined voice rang out in the tunnel.

'*Blow, friendly wind! Dispersio!*'

The hobgoblins shrank back as a twinkling of explosive stars lit up the dark tunnel.

'W-what's that noise?' stammered Trotter.

A low rumble, quiet at first, could be heard further along the passageway. A breeze fluttered around them.

'What have you done, you stupid frog?' yelled Spike.

The breeze turned into a wind, and the wind into a gale. It blew fiercely along the tunnel, swirling all around them. The hobgoblins flattened

themselves against the walls of the tunnel but it was no good. One by one, the wind lifted each one up and swirled them away, back along the tunnel to Hob Mountain.

'I did it!' croaked
Dave in wonder.

'You really did!
What a magician!'
cried Matty, lifting the
little frog up and giving him a kiss.

'A princess's kiss is magic. I should
really turn into a prince now,' said Dave,
blushing.

'I think we might have a problem,'
said Tansy, as the tunnel started to shake
around them.

'Cwumbs!'

Dust started to fall from the ceiling,

then rocks began to come loose, hitting the ground around them.

'The spell has weakened the tunnel! It's collapsing!'

CCCRRAASH!

Stones piled up all around them, and then as suddenly as the collapse had started, it stopped.

They each looked around at the dusty stones that now covered the floor of the tunnel, completely blocking the way out.

'How will we get out of here now?' Tansy asked fearfully.

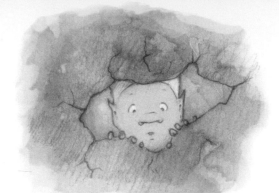

'Look!' cried Teasel, pointing up.
There was a large hole in the ceiling.
'Hello down there!' Mr Dollop's
kindly face looked down on them all.

'What a pickle you're in, my little cuckoo spit,' said Mr Dollop, reaching his big arm in to pull Matty out through the hole.

'Thanks, Mr Dollop. Could you reach Smoky too?' said Matty, carefully hiding the little frog in her pocket.

'Up you come, little dragon.'

The two fairies flew around Matty's head. 'We'd better get back to Raven Wood, Matty, and let Fern know we're safe.'

'Yes, go quickly. Goodbye, Teasel! Goodbye, Tansy!' Matty whispered into

the dark. 'Thanks for all your help!'

Mr Dollop, his armour clanking, continued his patrol of the castle grounds. 'I don't know why the King was so worried. I haven't had a sniff of a hobgoblin all night.

'THIRTEEN O'CLOCK AND ALL'S SMELL!'

Matty cuddled Smoky to her. 'It's all right now. We're safe. Are you okay?'

'Wight as wain,' nodded the little dragon.

 86

'Okey-smoky! Then we have a party to get back to!'

In the very top bedroom of the Goblin Castle, Matty woke late the next morning. The sun was already streaming in through the window. She looked down and smiled. Dave lay snoring, stretched out on his back between Smoky's paws. The little frog was still wearing his magician's hat.

'Matty! Matty!' There were three
fairies knocking at her bedroom
window, and all of them were smiling.

Matty flung the
window open and
Fern, Teasel and
Tansy all flew
in, happy to be
together again.

'So this is Dave.
Teasel and Tansy told me all about him.'
Fern flew down to perch on Smoky's
head so that she could take a closer
look at the sleeping frog.

'I think all those magic tricks exhausted him. He's very tired,' said Matty.

'Will he have to go back to the circus?' asked Teasel.

Matty stroked the little sleeping frog's head. 'No! Mr Froggit was a terrible owner. I asked my parents last night. Mum loves the idea of a slimy frog in the house. All I have to do now is ask Dave.'

'Fwog waking, Smatty!'

Dave opened an eye, yawned, and smiled at the assembled group

looking down at him. 'Good morning, everyone! I've just had such a lovely dream: I dreamt I really *did* turn into a prince.'

'Well, it's funny you should say that, Dave,' said Matty. 'Would you like to live in the castle, with me and Smoky?'

'With you? A princess? Then my dream has come true!' said Dave, his eyes shining in wonder.

'Yes!' laughed Matty. 'You'll have a new home and I'll have a brand-new friend. My very own frog prince!'

Make a
Goblin Feast!

Bat
Blamanche

Key slime
pie

Have your own Goblin Ball
with these fiendish recipes for
Scary Potato Faces,
Ghoulish Goblin Drinks
and Peppermint Cream Bugs!

slug
pate

Mice
cakes

Scary Potato Faces

You'll need . . .

- a large baked potato
- green food colouring
- 50g butter
- 50g grated cheese
- a carrot

- a red pepper
- spring onions
- a cooked sausage
- and an adult
  to help!

- Cut the top off your cooled baked potato. Scoop out its insides and mix them with the green food colouring, butter and some cheese.

- Spoon the mixture back into the potato.

- Make a face using the sausage, carrot, red pepper and onion. The rest of the cheese will make a scary hairstyle.

Ghoulish Goblin Drinks

You'll need . . .

- ice cream
- sparkling water
- lime juice
- a fun straw
- and an adult to help!

- Put some ice cream in a glass.

- Pour a mixture of the sparkling water and lime juice over the ice cream so that it froths up.

- Pop a fun ghoulish goblin straw in the glass. Enjoy!

Peppermint Cream Bugs

You'll need . . .

- 1 egg white
- 400g sifted icing sugar
- a few drops of green food colouring
- greaseproof paper

- 3 drops of peppermint extract
- dark or milk chocolate to melt
- and an adult to help!

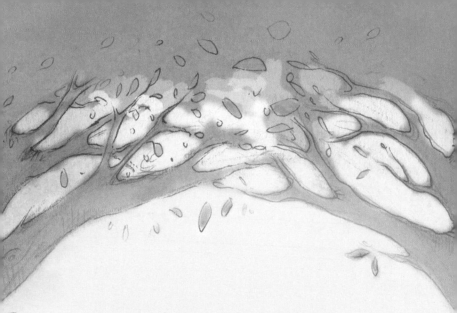

- Whisk the egg white, food colouring and peppermint together. Slowly stir in the icing sugar until it forms a dough.

- Roll out balls of the dough and press them flat on to the greaseproof paper. Use a fork to create ridges in each bug. Place in the fridge for about an hour to firm up.

- Melt the chocolate. Dip the top of each bug into the chocolate and leave them to set.

- Add two eyes with white icing.

Now have a Goblin Ball!

Have you read the first
Goblin Princess
adventure?

Everything is topsy-turvy in goblin world. And Matty, the Goblin Princess, doesn't fit in! The Goblin Queen is always telling her to untidy her room and eat up her slug porridge (yee-uk!) and to stay away from the Forest Fairies . . .

But Matty may just need the fairies' help to persuade her parents that her baby dragon is ~~good~~ naughty enough to keep!

COMING SOON . . .

The Snow Fairy

Growing up with
FABER